Munch Your Lunch!

Adapted by Becky Friedman

Based on the screenplays "Daniel Goes to School" written by Angela C. Santomero
and "Line Leader Daniel" written by Jennifer Hamburg

Poses and layouts by Jason Fruchter

Simon Spotlight
An imprint of Simon & Schuster Children's Publishing Division
New York   London   Toronto   Sydney   New Delhi
1230 Avenue of the Americas, New York, New York 10020
This Simon Spotlight paperback edition May 2018
© 2018 The Fred Rogers Company
For information about special discounts for bulk purchases, please contact Simon & Schuster Special Sales
at 1-866-506-1949 or business@simonandschuster.com.
Manufactured in the United States of America 0318 LAK   10 9 8 7 6 5 4 3 2 1
ISBN 978-1-5344-1778-6 • ISBN 978-1-5344-1779-3 (eBook)

It was a beautiful day in the neighborhood, and Daniel's dad was dropping him off at school.

"Guess what, Dad?" said Daniel. "Today we're getting our classroom jobs."

"That's exciting," said Dad Tiger. "I wonder what your job will be."

Inside his classroom, Dad Tiger gave Daniel his lunch box.

"Here's your lunch, Daniel," said Dad Tiger. "I put a surprise in it for later."

"You did?" said Daniel. "What is it?"

"You have to wait until lunch to find out!" Dad Tiger chuckled. "Now it's time for you to play. I'll see you after school!"

"Okay," said Daniel. "Bye, Dad!"

Miss Elaina walked over to Daniel Tiger . . . backward. "Daniel, guess what classroom job I want to have?"

"I don't know!" said Daniel.

"Backward helper!" Miss Elaina giggled. "Except that's not really a job."

"I want to be line leader," said Daniel.

It was circle time, and Teacher Harriet began to tell everyone what their classroom jobs were going to be.

Lights helper was . . . Katerina Kittycat!

Plant helper was . . . O the Owl! "Hoo hoo, yay!"

Snowball the bunny's helper was . . . Prince Wednesday!

And line leader was . . . Miss Elaina!

"Miss Elaina is line leader?" asked Daniel. "But . . . what's my job?"

"Daniel, your job is lunch helper," said Teacher Harriet. "You will pass out all of the lunch boxes at lunchtime."

"I don't want to be lunch helper," Daniel said sadly. "I want to be line leader."

Circle time was over, and everyone got up to do their jobs. Everyone was excited . . . except for Daniel.

It was lunchtime, and everyone was hungry.

"It's time to munch your lunch," Teacher Harriet said.

"I'm rrroyally hungry!" said Prince Wednesday.

"Me too! Hoo hoo," said O the Owl. "But where are our lunches?"

Daniel remembered that he was the lunch helper. Nobody could eat their lunch because he didn't do his job!

"Being lunch helper is an important job!" said Daniel. "Without me there's no lunch!"

Daniel gave his friends their lunch boxes.
Daniel gave the book lunch box to O the Owl and the Museum-Go-Round lunch box to Miss Elaina.

Daniel gave the royal crown lunch box to Prince Wednesday and the ballet lunch box with the pink ribbon on it to Katerina Kittycat.

At last, Daniel sat down with his tiger lunch box. "I wonder what I have for lunch today?" he said.

Daniel opened up his lunch. On top of the food he found a note! It was from Dad Tiger and said:

No matter what your classroom job is, you are special to me!
Ugga Mugga! Love, Dad Tiger

Daniel loved his dad's lunch box note, and he loved being lunch helper, too!

"What do you like to eat for lunch?" asks Daniel.

"Ugga Mugga!"

No matter what your classroom job is, you are special to me! Ugga Mugga! Love, Dad Tiger